WHEN
WILLARD MET
BABE RUTH

WHEN WILLARD MET BABE RUTH

A STORY BY
Donald Hall

ILLUSTRATED BY
Barry Moser

Voyager Books
Harcourt, Inc.

SAN DIEGO   NEW YORK   LONDON

www.harcourt.com

First Voyager Books edition 2001
Voyager Books is a trademark of Harcourt, Inc., registered in the
United States of America and other jurisdictions.

The Library of Congress has cataloged the hardcover edition as follows:
Hall, Donald, 1928–
When Willard met Babe Ruth/by Donald Hall; illustrated by Barry Moser.
p.   cm.
Summary: A boy meets the young Babe Ruth and along with his family
follows the Babe's long and illustrious career.
1. Ruth, Babe, 1895–1948—Juvenile fiction. [1. Ruth, Babe, 1895–1948—Fiction.
2. Baseball—Fiction.] I. Moser, Barry, ill. II. Title.
PZ7.H14115Ba1   1996
[Fic]—dc20   94-30798
ISBN 0-15-200273-1
ISBN 0-15-202477-8 pb

H G F E D C B A

The paintings in this book were done

in transparent watercolor on handmade Barcham Green paper.

The hand-lettering is by Georgia Deaver.

The text type was set in Trump Mediaeval by Thompson Type, San Diego, California.

Color separations by Bright Arts, Ltd., Singapore

Printed and bound by Tien Wah Press, Singapore

This book was printed on Arctic matte paper.

Production supervision by Sandra Grebenar and Pascha Gerlinger

Designed by Barry Moser

To Andrew and Philippa
D. H.

For Willie Morris
—B. M.

1.

WILLARD BABSON LOVED the Fourth of July. In the morning he watched the parade and at night there were fireworks, but best was the afternoon baseball game between the married men and the single men of Wilmot Flat in New Hampshire.

In 1917, when Willard was twelve, his father Sheridan pitched left-handed and beat the single men, 14 to 10. After the game, his father, his mother Edna, and Willard each ate an ice-cream cone.

Every Fourth of July, they ate ice-cream cones.

All summer Willard and his father brought in the hay. It was just the two of them, now that Willard's big brother had left home. Sheridan perched on the mowing machine, behind Stonewall the horse, while Willard trimmed the edges of the field with a scythe.

They worked all morning. At noon the RFD man brought the mail in his buggy, so that Sheridan could read in the *Boston Post* about what the plaguey Republicans were up to. Willard enjoyed hearing his father, who was one of the few Democrats in New Hampshire, grumble about politics.

In the *Post,* Willard and his father read about games played by the Boston baseball teams. Boston was the capital city of baseball; four years in the last five, a Boston team had won the World Series.

"It's a shame the Braves are so bad this year," said Sheridan.

"Sixth place!" said Willard. "But the Red Sox have got Babe Ruth."

"We've got the best young pitcher in baseball." Sheridan nodded. "The best left-hander."

Last year, when the Red Sox had won the World Series, twenty-one-year-old Babe Ruth had pitched a shutout. In the 1917 season, he won twenty-four games and hit two home runs—but the Red Sox came in only second in the American League.

The hay was in, the cattle were still pasturing, Willard was back in school, and Sheridan readied the farm for winter. Time to move the pullets in with the hens. Time to pen the geese. Time to bring the sheep from pasture to their winter quarters in the sheep barn.

One day after school, Willard, Sheridan, and Meg the sheepdog drove the flock along the dirt road of Old Highway Number 4. From the barnyard two geese and a gander rushed at the ewes. They baaed and backed nervously into the road.

"Sheep are dumb," said Sheridan. "It always surprises me, how dumb sheep are!"

"And geese are fierce!" said Willard. "A goose would fight a lion!"

Then they heard the clattering noise of an automobile roaring along the dirt road. A huge cloud of dust with a shiny grille at the front of it bore down on their flock. Willard waved his arms, the driver screeched his brakes, and the big roadster slid sideways into the ditch.

Willard murmured to soothe a frightened ewe; Meg rounded up two lambs. When Willard walked back to the roadster, his father was talking to the tall young driver. A pretty woman sat tilted in the front seat, arranging her hat.

"It's okay," said the young man, inspecting his car. "No busted axle or nothing. Sorry I was going so damned—darned—fast. You know anybody can pull me out of here?"

Willard's father looked hard at the man. "I'll get my oxen," he said. "We'll pull you out, no time . . . You been resting up after the season?"

"Yup," said Babe Ruth, "down by Canobie Lake. Hunting and fishing, mostly." He put his hand out. "Pleased to meet you. This here's my wife, Helen."

While his father trotted to the barn to fetch Grant and Sherman the oxen, Willard kept one eye on the sheep and geese, who were getting reacquainted, and with his other eye he stared at the best left-hander in baseball.

Meg took after Felix the gander, who had wandered off.

3

"Gol, those are big ducks," said the Babe.

"Geese," said Willard. "My father pitches left-handed."

"You a pitcher too, kid?" asked the Babe.

Willard told about playing with five boys in a cut hayfield. "We take turns playing all the positions," he said. "We've got my father's bat that he turned on his own lathe. We've got a ball my brother sent from Idaho. We don't need a glove."

Mrs. Ruth opened the car door and stepped out, her husband helping her. Then the Babe knelt to look under the car again.

As Meg tried driving the gander into the sheep yard, Felix rushed honking at Mrs. Ruth, who gave a little scream and jumped backward. Willard leapt in front of her, grabbed Felix, got his hand pecked, and shoved the gander into the yard, shutting the gate.

Mrs. Ruth put her hand to her throat. "Thank you!" she said to Willard. "Thank you!"

"That's some duck!" said the Babe. "Did he hurt you, kid?" he asked Willard.

"No," said Willard, rubbing his hand. "They're geese."

"Kid, you catch baseballs the way you catch ducks, pretty soon we'll be playing together."

Then Sheridan led his oxen down from the barn,

hitched a chain to the roadster, and pulled it out of the ditch. The car started, and Mr. and Mrs. Ruth prepared to drive back to Canobie Lake. But first Babe Ruth reached into the rumble seat.

"Kid," he said, tossing it to Willard, "now you got a glove."

2.

THE WAR IN EUROPE filled the *Boston Post,* winter and spring of 1918. In the tie-up, while Sheridan milked his seven Holsteins before supper, Willard and his father talked about the trenches of France. "I'm glad you're too young for the AEF," said Sheridan.

Willard knew that President Wilson was right, and that American boys would set things straight over there, but really he was more interested in baseball. He made sure that his father recited Willard's favorite poem, "Casey at the Bat," at least once a week.

Willard took the Babe's glove to school with him, but when he wouldn't let go of it during penmanship his

teacher, Miss Heatherington, asked him not to bring it anymore.

At night his mother sewed and his father read. When his father went *"Humph,"* Willard knew that someone in the paper was criticizing President Wilson.

While Willard studied his lessons, reading with his schoolbook flat on the table under the oil lamp, he pounded his big brother's baseball into the mitt in his lap.

Last thing at night, they fed the cows, oxen, horse, and sheep, and put up the geese and chickens. Walking back to the house for bed, they talked about next year's baseball—and about Babe Ruth of the Boston Red Sox.

Willard took the Babe's glove to bed with him, along with his hot-water bottle.

After a big thaw and one small March blizzard, snowdrops blossomed, daffodils bloomed, grass greened, and sheep and cattle went to pasture. Sheridan took the time, between milking and shutting up the geese, to play catch with Willard. When school was over and they weren't hoeing or haying with their fathers, Willard and his friends played pasture baseball. Willard owned the glove.

At noontime every day, the *Post* told them that the Braves were worse than last year, but the news from the Red Sox about Babe Ruth was amazing. He hit *eleven* home runs in 1918. The most "Home Run" Baker had ever hit was twelve, and Baker played every day.

The Babe started to play first base or left field when he wasn't pitching. Sheridan said to Willard, "It looks as if your friend the best left-handed pitcher in baseball might turn out to be the best hitter!"

One noontime Willard's father read a letter out loud. In July President Wilson would visit Boston to speak at a Liberty Bond rally, and Sheridan Babson, as a leading New Hampshire Democrat, was invited to attend the rally—8:00 P.M. on the evening of July 17. Willard was proud of his father.

Later, in his room, he looked at a baseball schedule. The Red Sox were playing a doubleheader with the St. Louis Browns on Wednesday, July 17, 1918.

Willard saw his mother and father close the pantry door to talk. When the door opened, he watched Edna lift a half dollar out of the china pitcher on the highest shelf. Bleacher seats cost twenty-five cents.

Sheridan found someone to do the 5:00 P.M. milking and feed the creatures. Edna took Willard and Sheridan to the depot with Stonewall pulling the buggy. The 9:00 A.M. train got to North Station at 11:30, plenty of time.

A trolley car to Fenway Park rattled past one million people walking on a Wednesday noontime, past one million buildings each a mile high.

Sheridan and Willard watched Boston win the first game, 7 to 0. Babe Ruth, playing left field, hit a single and made a sprinting catch of a line drive. Everyone stood up to cheer.

Then, in the second game, the Babe was starting pitcher. He had not pitched lately—because (the paper said) he hit more when he didn't pitch—but his team needed him, so he moved from the outfield to the pitcher's mound.

When Babe Ruth warmed up between games, between the right field stands and the foul line, Willard and his father walked to where they could watch him.

"See how his pitches break more sharply as he warms up?" Sheridan said.

Willard nodded.

The Babe was ready. He stopped throwing and wiped the sweat from his forehead. Looking around, he saw Willard and Sheridan above him. He looked puzzled, turned away, and then looked back. He smiled at Willard.

"Hey, kid. Aren't you the kid with that big duck in New Hampshire?"

"You gave me your glove," said Willard. "It was a gander."

"This's to go with the glove, kid," said the Babe, flipping Willard his warm-up ball as he strode toward the mound.

That afternoon, Babe Ruth pitched like the best left-hander in baseball, and he batted cleanup as well. He hit a double off the left-field wall in the second, driving in a run. He hit another double in the fifth, drove in another run, and scored.

"The Colossus"—as the newspaper called him—went 3 for 6 in the doubleheader and pitched a 4–0 shutout in the second game, which ended when rain flooded out the sixth inning.

Sheridan and Willard were soaked through when they listened to President Wilson give an excellent talk in Mechanix Hall. Willard dozed off, and his father had to wake him for the last sleepy train to Wilmot Depot.

They walked home to the farm in the rainy dark. In his pants pocket, Willard kept his baseball dry.

3.

ON LABOR DAY the single men beat the married men. Sheridan lost the pitchers' battle, 11 to 9.

But the Red Sox won the pennant. Then they beat the Chicago Cubs, 4 games to 2, to win the World Series.

Babe Ruth was a pitcher again, throwing a shutout in the first game, 1–0.

He won the fourth game of the Series, giving up a run in the eighth—but only after pitching a record number of consecutive scoreless World Series innings.

The United States won the war, Wilmot Flat celebrated, and November 11 was like a Fourth of July with the leaves down.

With the boys coming home and the Red Sox champions, Willard could concentrate on baseball. Sheridan milked in the tie-up and recited "Casey at the Bat." He was getting ready for a golden wedding anniversary when he would speak pieces for entertainment.

Edna wasn't a reciter, but she made up rhymes for the Grange or Old Home Day if they needed a poem for a celebration.

When the 4-H Club offered a prize for "Best Young Person's Poem," Willard remembered July's double-header. He scribbled in his schoolbook at night while he was supposed to be memorizing the principal products of Portugal. He thought of rhymes when he walked home from school.

One night just before bedtime, he stood before his mother and father like an umpire and said, "Play ball!"

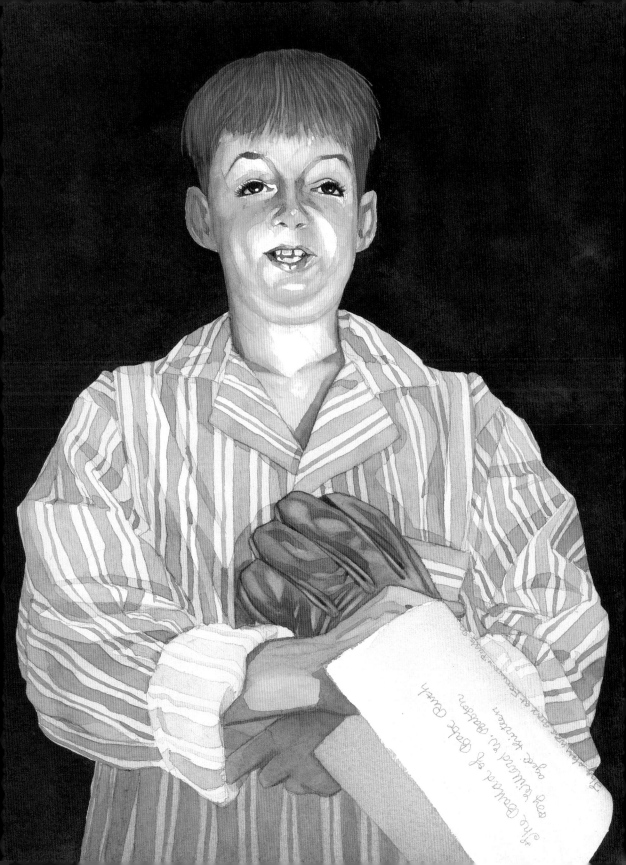

He recited, "This is 'The Ballad of Babe Ruth.'

"The sky was gray at Fenway Park on seventeen July.

We watched the Red Sox play two games under a cloudy sky.

Left fielder for the first of two, a lanky man named Ruth,

Sprinted to catch a low line drive and caught the ball, in truth.

Then when the second game began, fans were amazed to see

Left fielder turned to pitcher—George Herman Ruth was he.

He struck them out or popped them up, the Babe was in command,

And then he knocked two runs in—hero of Fenway land!

The pitcher batted cleanup and gave St. Louis trouble.

He hit a double first time up. Next time he hit a double.

He pitched five innings shutout, stopped only by the rain.

My dad and I were sopping wet when we got off the train."

When Willard finished, Sheridan allowed that it was "a fine piece of work for a boy of thirteen."

Edna said that she bet he would win the prize, and asked him to write out a copy. Two weeks later Willard saw his poem printed in the weekly *Franklin Transcript*, "by Willard W. Babson, aged thirteen." From the 4-H Club he won a subscription to *Youth's Companion*.

Next summer the Red Sox came in sixth, but Babe Ruth hit twenty-nine home runs, more than anybody had ever hit in the history of baseball. That winter Edna cut "The Ballad of Babe Ruth" from an extra copy of the paper and mailed it to "George Herman Ruth, c/o the Boston Red Sox, Fenway Park, Boston, Massachusetts." She mailed the letter on January 6. That same day the *Post* ran a headline:

Babe Ruth Sold to Yankees

4.

IT WAS DIFFICULT TO LOVE Babe Ruth but hate the Yankees, who won everything.

The Red Sox came in last for nine years out of eleven. In the National League, the Braves were almost as hopeless.

These were the years when the prices of milk and wool went down, down, down. Small farms went into a depression before the rest of the country. Sheridan worked harder than ever. Willard helped, and he hired out after school at harvest.

In 1921, when he was sixteen, Willard quit school to work—hours in the forge, repairing sap buckets; hours setting out new apple trees in the orchard; hours clearing a brushy meadow to sow clover. The cows loved clover and made more milk.

In 1920 Babe Ruth hit fifty-four home runs, and in 1921, fifty-nine.

In 1922 Willard pitched for the single men against the married men and lost to his father, 19–14. Sometimes on Sunday afternoons, Sheridan and Willard played baseball together—taking turns pitching and catching— for Wilmot Flat against Andover Plains or Danbury Bog.

In 1923 Sheridan turned his ankle sliding into second base. Next year Sheridan and Edna watched Willard pitch for the single men.

In 1924 Babe Ruth hit forty-six home runs. Sheridan and Edna moved into the cottage down the road where the farmhand used to live. Willard took over the big old house, because Willard, now called Will, had married Janet Colby from Miss Heatherington's school. Next year their daughter Ruth was born.

In 1927 Babe Ruth hit sixty home runs. Now everybody knew that Babe Ruth was the best who ever played the game.

Will was teased to say "The Ballad of Babe Ruth" at the Grange Harvest Festival Potluck in Danbury. Two-year-old Ruthie clapped when he finished. It must have been pat-a-cake.

After dinner every noontime, Will took the newspaper down to his mother and father. They talked about baseball. Then Will and Sheridan talked about how the plaguey Republicans were ruining the country.

In 1928, Fourth of July, Sheridan and Edna watched with Janet and Ruthie as Will pitched the first shutout in the history of Wilmot Flat baseball. The married men won, 21–0.

That election year, there was a picture in the paper of Babe Ruth wearing a bowler hat, with a sign pinned on his coat reading VOTE FOR AL SMITH. Smith was run-

ning for president as a Democrat against Herbert Hoover. Sheridan tacked the picture to his icebox.

That year, Will started doing a weekly column of Wilmot Flat news for the *Franklin Transcript*—$1.75 every week plus a free subscription. It helped.

When Ruthie was five years old, she laughed while tossing balled socks back and forth with her father. Will told her about the man she was named for. He showed her an old glove and an old baseball. He told about Grandpa's oxen pulling Babe Ruth's roadster out of the ditch. He told about Felix, "the big duck."

When Babe Ruth got a raise in salary in 1931, somebody asked him how it felt to make more money than President Hoover. "Why not? I had a better year than he did," said the Babe.

Sheridan and Willard repeated that story to each other every day.

In 1932 Will wrote an editorial twice a month for the *Transcript* for five dollars a column.

All summer Ruthie asked what Babe Ruth had done the day before. Will read aloud to her from the sports page.

During the World Series that year, the papers were full of the Babe again. They said that he pointed to a place in center field and hit a home run right where he pointed.

Sheridan shook his head, grinning, when Will told him the latest Babe Ruth story. "What'll he do next?"

Besides local news and editorials, sometimes Will wrote about sports for the *Transcript*. Two or three afternoons at the *Transcript* office made him ten dollars every week.

Instead of pitching, now Will wrote about baseball. Sheridan, Edna, Janet, Will, and Ruthie sat under an elm and watched the game.

In 1934 at Sheridan and Edna's fortieth anniversary, Will recited "Casey at the Bat." When Edna asked him, he said "The Ballad of Babe Ruth" for an encore.

Ruthie learned to sew.

She also learned her namesake's batting average and home-run records.

In 1934 Babe Ruth hit only twenty-two home runs, with a .288 batting average. Not very good for Babe Ruth. People said he was too old, at thirty-nine, for the game of baseball.

Ruthie went to the same one-room East Wilmot school her father had gone to. When she was almost ten, she was named best reciter, in prize speaking, doing "Casey at the Bat."

Then they read in the *Post* that Babe Ruth was leaving the New York Yankees for the Boston Braves.

5.

THAT WINTER, in the cold middle of the Great Depression, Will became managing editor of the *Transcript* at twenty dollars a week. The family felt rich. The job took him only three days and part of a fourth, so he could keep two cows, ten sheep, thirty chickens, and one goose.

In their blue Chevrolet, they drove to Franklin on Saturday nights and watched *Mutiny on the Bounty* and *Ruggles of Red Gap.*

That winter they bought an Arrow cabinet radio and listened to "Your Hit Parade" and "Fibber McGee and Molly."

Will said to Ruthie, "You know, when baseball starts, we'll hear the scores on the six o'clock news, the same day as the game!"

Janet and Will listened to political news. The Supreme Court overturned a Roosevelt program, and they both went *"Humph."*

Ruthie would turn ten on April 16, 1935, and this year there was mystery about her birthday. Edna, Sheridan, Will, and Janet smiled secret smiles. Even her teacher at school, when she went home the afternoon before, seemed to know something.

"See you tomorrow," said Ruth to Miss Heatherington.

"See you *soon*," said Miss Heatherington, as if she were correcting a spelling error.

At home the family gathered in the living room, and Ruthie found that she was getting her presents a day early. She opened packages first: two new books and a sweater from her Idaho cousins. She opened a small square box to find a beautiful new wooden darning egg from Edna and Sheridan that Sheridan himself had turned on his lathe. Edna had rheumatism these days, but if Ruthie would come down to the cottage, Edna would teach her to darn.

Then Janet disappeared for a moment and returned with a white cake decorated with lines of red icing to look like the stitches on a baseball. Around the rim of the cake there were ten candles, and in the center, tucked into the frosting, was a narrow brown envelope.

Ruthie blew out the candles and looked at her mother and father.

"Open it up," said Will.

When she pulled out three tickets, she knew: Tomorrow was opening day at Braves Field, and Ruthie held in her hand three box seats for the baseball game that was to be Babe Ruth's return to Boston.

She made a noise like the air swooshing from a balloon.

"We take the eleven o'clock train," said her father. "Your grandfather makes three."

"Miss Heatherington says it's all right," her mother said, "because you're such a good scholar."

"I'll cook," said her grandmother. "Your mother will milk the cows."

"I never thought," said Sheridan, "we'd ever see Babe Ruth again."

Ruthie's first trip to Boston reminded Will of his trip almost twenty years before. "I bet it's the same locomotive," Will said to Sheridan.

The same trolley car with the same conductor took them to Braves Field instead of Fenway Park. They arrived at one-forty-five for the three o'clock game. It was cold, but they sat in the sun.

After they sat watching practice for ten minutes while substitutes took turns at bat, Will suggested that they walk around under the stadium before the game. Sheridan fetched a dime from his trousers and bought Ruthie a scorecard, which she tucked into a coat pocket.

Father, daughter, and grandfather walked under the stadium until they came to a door marked PRESS with a policeman in front of it.

Will took a card from his side pocket and showed it to the policeman. "Press," said Will. "*Franklin Transcript.*"

The policeman smiled and started to open the door. Then he saw Ruthie and Sheridan. "Sorry," he said. "Nobody else."

Will spoke rapidly: "It's her birthday. She's named Ruth, after your left fielder. And this's her grandfather. He pulled Mr. Ruth's car out of a ditch."

The policeman turned away so that he didn't actually see a family, including a ten-year-old girl and a seventy-year-old man, enter through the press door.

No one was there. Will pointed out the clippings on the wall. "I know we won't see him," he said, "but we're *close*."

The door opened and Babe Ruth clanked in, wearing cleats, sweaty from batting practice. He was forty years old and fat. He looked tired, not like the strong young athlete Will and Sheridan had met in 1917.

Ruthie squeezed her father's hand and took a deep breath.

"Who's the kid?" said Babe Ruth. "Hi, kid. I was supposed to see some guy from some magazine."

Will said, "It's her birthday. Her name is Ruth, named after you."

"I'll be damned," said the Babe. "Darned."

Ruthie said, "My dad and my grandfather pulled your roadster out of a ditch with oxen."

"Huh?" said the Babe.

"That we did," said Sheridan, smiling broadly.

"You gave my dad your glove," said Ruthie, pulling the small old glove from her coat pocket.

"I'll be damned," said Babe Ruth. "Darned." He looked at Will. "Hey, were you that kid with the . . . goose?"

Will nodded and squeezed Ruthie's hand.

Nobody told Babe Ruth that Felix was a gander.

Sheridan said, "That roadster was surely a heavy car."

"Hey, kid," the Babe said, pointing at Ruthie's score-card, which was sticking out of her other coat pocket. "Give me that thing."

Babe Ruth wrote, "Happy Birthday from Ruth to Ruth." He said, "I got to talk to some guy from some magazine. If I hit one today, kid, it's for your birthday. Okay?"

While Ruthie and Will and Sheridan watched, the Boston Braves beat the New York Giants, 4 to 2, and Babe Ruth scored or drove in all four runs.

In the first inning, the old man hit a single that knocked a run in. Then he scored a run himself.

He struck out in the second, but in the fifth, with a man on base, the Babe hit a letter-high fastball on a 2 and 2 count that landed in the Braves Field stands.

It was his 709th home run, and it won the game.

He hit it off Carl Hubbell, who was now the best left-handed pitcher in baseball.

When Hubbell batted in the sixth inning, just after the Babe's homer, he hit a hard line drive over third base—but "the portly left fielder," as next morning's paper put it, "ran like a deer to make a diving catch of the line drive."

As the *Post* reported, "It was the defensive play of the game."

Ruthie, Will, and Sheridan napped on the train going home. They stretched, stepping down in the darkness at Wilmot Depot. The blue Chevy started right away.

As they drove up to the farm on the blacktop, Will said he kind of *missed* the dirt road.

"And roadsters that slide into ditches?" asked Ruthie.

"Definitely," said Sheridan, as Will parked the car by the farmhouse.

"And a gander named Felix," Will yawned.

Ruthie carried her signed scorecard into the kitchen. "I wish he still called him a big duck," she said.

"What an opening day!" Sheridan added. "They said he couldn't play anymore. The Babe's got a lot of baseball left in him."

But the Babe didn't have much more baseball left. The Boston Braves ended the 1935 season forty-seven games out of first place. One afternoon in Pittsburgh, a few weeks after opening day, Babe Ruth hit three home runs—but after that game, he never had another hit. His average dropped to .181. In May, he left the team and the game of baseball forever.

GEORGE HERMAN ("BABE") RUTH

Babe Ruth was born in 1895 and left the St. Mary's In-dustrial School in Baltimore to play minor league base-ball in 1914. A year later he began pitching for the Boston Red Sox, and in two World Series, he set a record for consecutive shutout innings. As a pitcher he won 94 games and lost only 46—but his bat turned him into a left fielder who could play and hit every day. From 1919 to 1921, he broke the home-run record each year. He led the league twelve times, hitting 40 and more home runs in eleven of his seasons, and in 1927 he hit 60. In his twenty-two years as a major leaguer, he had 2,873 hits, of which 714 were home runs. His average, in ten World Series, was .326.

Babe Ruth died in 1948. He was the best who ever played the game of baseball.